CONTENTS

The Library of Doom is a hidden fortress.
It holds the world's largest collection
of strange and dangerous books.

Behold the Librarian. He defends the Library – and
the world – from super-villains, clever thieves
and fierce monsters. Many of his adventures
have remained secret. Now they can be told.

SECRET #333

A BOOK CAN BE A WEAPON OR A SHIELD,
DEPENDING ON WHO HOLDS IT.

Chapter One

THE SECRET IN THE CLOUD

A small aeroplane **SOARS** above a sandy desert.

The sky is bright blue. Only one cloud floats in the WIDE sky.

The aeroplane flies towards the cloud and disappears into it.

Inside the cloud, the plane keeps flying. It is surrounded by white mist.

Then the mist **PARTS**.

A **HUGE** metal fortress hangs in the air.

It is hidden inside the cloud.

The aeroplane **SWOOPS** down towards a runway on the fortress.

ZZHHOOOOOOOOMM!

The plane lands in less than a minute.

The pilot **JUMPS** out of the plane.
He is carrying a small wooden chest.

A group of people run out of the
building to greet him.

A woman at the front SHAKES the pilot's hand.

"Did you find it?" she asks. "Did you find the Golden Book of Death?"

The pilot nods. "Yes, Captain. The book is inside this chest. But I can't open it," he says. "No HUMAN can."

Chapter Two

STORM WEAPON

"The chest was locked inside the TOWER of Gargoyles," the pilot says.

"I thought the Tower was just a legend," says the captain.

MMM-RRRR-MMM-RRRRMMM

A STRANGE humming fills the air.

"I've heard that sound before," says the pilot.

"We're under attack!" **SHOUTS** the captain. "Everyone into the Wing!"

Men and women rush inside the **METAL** fortress.

"Battle stations!" orders the captain.

The fortress is called the **WING**.
It is part of the Library of Doom.

The people who work there are the
Wing Warriors.

They **CIRCLE** the planet in the
fortress searching for dangerous books.

They also **DEFEND** the fortress against attacks.

The Warriors cannot let anyone steal the deadly books.

"I need Storm Control!" **SHOUTS** the captain. "Let's stop those attackers!"

Three Warriors climb up a **METAL** tower. They reach the control room that sits at the top.

"Lightning storm coming now!" says a Warrior. She **TURNS** a dial. "They won't get through this."

Outside the Wing fortress, the cloud turns dark.

KRRRR-AAKKKKK!

A bolt of lightning CRASHES through the air. Thunder rumbles.

Chapter Three

WING VS WINGS

The captain and the pilot watch the storm through a **TALL** window.

The Wing fortress floats in **DARKNESS**.

But when lightning flashes, they see a swarm of hundreds of **FLYING** creatures.

"Those are gargoyles from the Tower," says the pilot. "They've followed me!"

The gargoyles have TAILS like whips.

Bat-like wings **FLAP** from their shoulders. Their hands and feet are armed with sharp claws.

"The lightning isn't stopping them," says the captain. "We need something else!"

Up in the **TOWER**, the Warriors try another weapon.

"Blizzard power!" they cry.

The black cloud turns **GREY**.

Sheets of snow **SWEEP** through the air. Freezing winds shake the fortress.

The Wing Warriors can no longer see the attackers.

"We did it!" shouts the pilot. "The gargoyles have been blown away!"

Then they hear a SCRAPING sound.

SSKRRICH SSKRRICH SSKRRICH

Gargoyles are clawing at the outside door.

Chapter Four

GOLDEN BOOK OF DEATH

Warriors hurry to **PROTECT** the fortress's main door.

The pilot grips the chest. "The gargoyles cannot get the Golden Book."

The captain orders the Warriors in the tower, "Send an emergency signal to –"

GGWWOOOOOSHHHHHHHH!

The door caves in. A group of gargoyles **RUSHES** towards the Warriors.

The gargoyles flap their huge bat wings.
The wings create a powerful wind.

The Warriors are **BLOWN** off their feet.

The pilot falls. The chest tumbles from
his hands.

The **BIGGEST** gargoyle leaps across the floor and grabs the chest.

KRRRAAAAAAH!

The gargoyle **SHRIEKS** in triumph.

"You stole our treasure," it says.
"Now, you will feel the book's power!"

The gargoyle **TURNS** the lock on
the chest.

The captain whispers to the pilot,
"You said no one could open it."

"I said no *human* could open it," explains the pilot.

"The Golden Book will destroy you!" says the gargoyle.

The lid of the chest begins to **OPEN**.

A light SHINES from the small crack.

Chapter Five

NO HUMAN

Suddenly the fortress starts to SHAKE.
The floor between the gargoyles and the
Warriors rips open.

Snow and wind **SWIRL** into the hallway.

A man in a long coat and dark glasses
RISES up through the hole.

The Librarian stands between the Warriors and the gargoyles. The LIGHT only strikes the flying creatures.

The gargoyles turn to STONE.

Then they **CRUMBLE** apart and blow away in the cold, swirling wind.

The Librarian turns the chest back into wood. The light fades AWAY.

The Librarian **HANDS** the chest to the captain.

"No one, human or not, should find this book again," he says.

"We will **GUARD** it with our lives," says the captain.

The Wing Warriors all stand at attention. They salute the Librarian.

The hero nods and then soars out
into the sky.

GLOSSARY

chest a box for holding things and keeping them safe

fortress a place that is highly guarded and protected from attacks

gargoyle a strange, scary-looking beast made of stone; they are found on old buildings

shimmer to shine with a light that seems to move back and forth

signal something, such as a sound or motion, that gives a warning, command or other piece of information

swarm a group of animals flying or moving together

warrior a person who fights in battle and shows courage and skill

wing a building that is an add-on to a larger main building

TALK ABOUT IT

1. How do you think the pilot felt when he saw the swarm of gargoyles? Why? How would you have felt?

2. Were you surprised when the Librarian came to help the Wing Warriors fight off the attackers? Why or why not?

WRITE ABOUT IT

1. Write the story of how the pilot first got the Golden Book. What challenges did he face at the Tower of Gargoyles? Make sure you make the story exciting!

2. Imagine a new flying foe that the Wing Warriors must battle. List its powers and describe what it looks like. Then draw a picture.

ABOUT THE AUTHOR

Michael Dahl is an award-winning author of more than 200 books for young people. He especially likes to write scary or weird fiction. His latest series are the sci-fi adventure Escape from Planet Alcatraz and School Bus of Horrors. As a child, Michael spent lots of time in libraries. "The creepier, the better," he says. These days, besides writing, he likes travelling and hunting for the one, true door that leads to the Library of Doom.

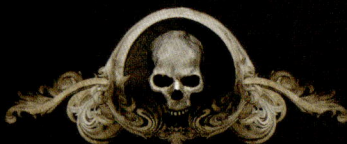

ABOUT THE ILLUSTRATOR

Patricio Clarey was born in Argentina. He graduated in fine arts from the Martín A. Malharro School of Visual Arts, specializing in illustration and graphic design. Patricio currently lives in Barcelona, Spain, where he works as a freelance graphic designer and illustrator. He has created several comics and graphic novels, and his work has been featured in books and other publications.